A Tail of Two Kitties

This book belongs to

Once I was very small

Written &
illustrated by
Elizabeth Ferber

Annick Press

Design by Sheryl Shapiro

Annick Press Ltd.

Annick Press gratefully acknowledges the support of the Canada Council and the Ontario Arts Council.

Canadian Cataloguing in Publication Data

Ferber, Elizabeth, 1953-
  Once I was very small

ISBN 1-5037-318-8 (bound) ISBN 1-55037-321-8 (pbk.)

I. Title.

PS8561.E72062 1993   jC813'.54   C93-093429-6
PZ.F37On 1993

The art in this book was rendered in pen and ink and watercolour. The text was typeset in Avalon.

Distributed in Canada by:
Firefly Books Ltd.
250 Sparks Ave.
Willowdale, ON M2H 2S4

Distributed in the U.S.A. by:
Firefly Books Ltd.
P.O. Box 1325
Ellicott Station
Buffalo, NY 14205

∞ Printed on acid-free paper.

Printed and bound in Canada by
D.W. Friesen & Sons, Altona, Manitoba.

For Tom Willard

Hi, I'm Vanessa.

Once I was very small,

so small that I could
fit into a shoebox.

Not anymore...

I'll show you.

In this picture I was just a baby,
sitting in a grown-up sized chair.

Now I fit this chair just right.

When I was very small I got so
many things, just for being born.

The snowsuit was my favourite...
it had a life of its own.

My grandma gave
me a ballet outfit.
One day I will dance.

These shoes were really big
and now they fit me fine.

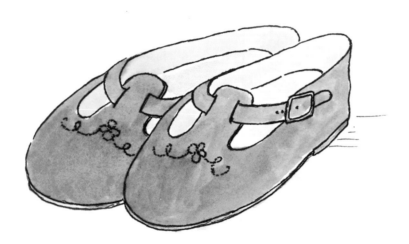

Look how much I've grown.

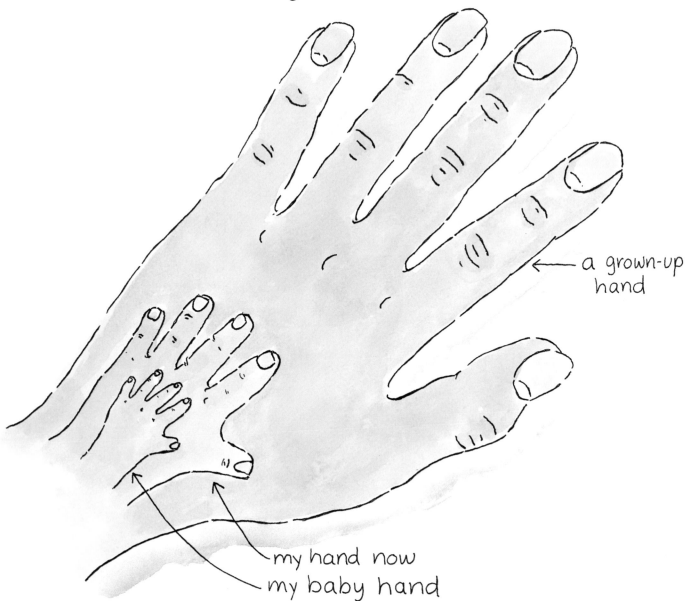

a grown-up hand

my hand now
my baby hand

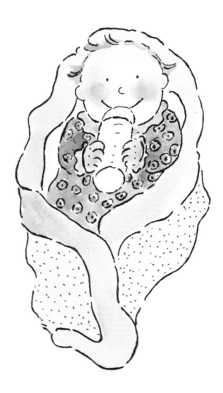

For a long time
I drank only milk,
which I loved...

...until I tasted grown-up food.

I also grew teeth,
which was good timing.

I have not tasted everything
yet, but I'm working on it.

Being very small has its ups

and downs

Then I began walking...

come
to daddy

over here
Vanessa

which really helped me get around.

And then something wonderful happened —
Christmas.
It comes once a year,

along with lots of other good things...
... like birthdays

... and friends to share them with.